Is it Time?

by Marilyn Janovitz

North-South Books

New York | London

For Daphne and Tomtor

Published in the United States by North-South Books Inc., New York.

Published simultaneously in Great Britain, Canada,
Australia, and New Zealand in 1994 by North-South Books,
an imprint of Nord-Süd Verlag AG, Gossau Zürich, Switzerland.

Library of Congress Cataloging-in-Publication Data
Janovitz, Marilyn.
Is it time? / by Marilyn Janovitz.
Summary: Rhyming questions and answers
lead a young wolf from bath into bed.
[1. Wolves—Fiction. 2. Baths—Fiction. 3. Bedtime—Fiction.
4. Sleep—Fiction. 5. Stories in rhyme.] I. Title.
ISBN 1-55858-331-9 (trade binding)
ISBN 1-55858-332-7 (library binding)
PZ8.3.J2631S 1994
(E)—DC20 94-5100

British Library Cataloguing in Publication Data is available

1 3 5 7 9 TB 10 8 6 4 2
1 3 5 7 9 LB 10 8 6 4 2
Printed in Belgium

*The illustrations in this book were created
with colored pencil and watercolor.*

Is it time to run the tub?

Yes, it's time to run the tub.

Is it time to rub-a-dub-dub?

Yes, it's time to rub-a-dub-dub.

Run the tub, rub-a-dub-dub.

Is it time to use the towel?

Yes, it's time to use the towel.

Is it time to give a howl?

Yes, it's time to give a howl.

Use the towel, give a howl,
Run the tub, rub-a-dub-dub.

Is it time to brush my fangs?

Yes, it's time to brush your fangs.

Is it time to comb my bangs?

Yes, it's time to comb your bangs.

Brush my fangs, comb my bangs,
Use the towel, give a howl,
Run the tub, rub-a-dub-dub.

Is it time to dress for bed?

Yes, it's time to dress for bed.

Is it time to tuck in Ted?

Yes, it's time to tuck in Ted.

Dress for bed, tuck in Ted,
Brush my fangs, comb my bangs,
Use the towel, give a howl,
Run the tub, rub-a-dub-dub.

Is it time to kiss good night?

Yes, it's time to kiss good night.

Is it time to switch the light?

Yes, it's time to switch the light.

Kiss good night, switch the light,
Dress for bed, tuck in Ted,
Brush my fangs, comb my bangs,
Use the towel, give a howl,
Run the tub, rub-a-dub-dub.

Is it time to go to sleep?

Yes, it's time to go to sleep.

Go to sleep and dream of sheep.